THE GUM ON THE DRUM

WRITTEN BY
BARBARA GREGORICH

ILLUSTRATED BY
JOHN SANDFORD

The bear likes gum.

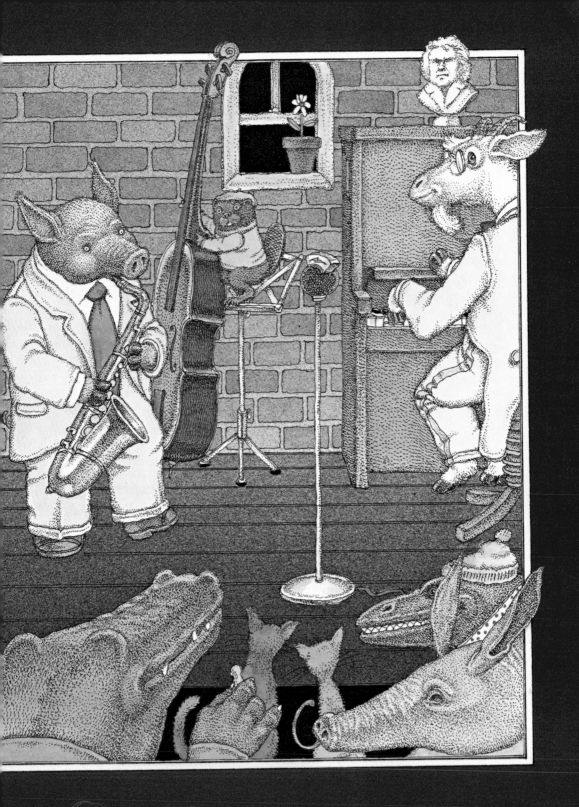

The bear plays the drum.

The bear wants to hum.

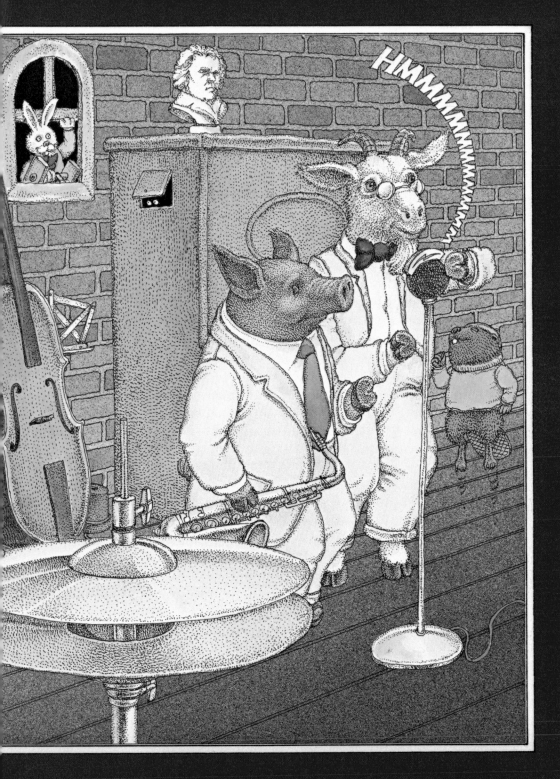

But he cannot hum with gum.

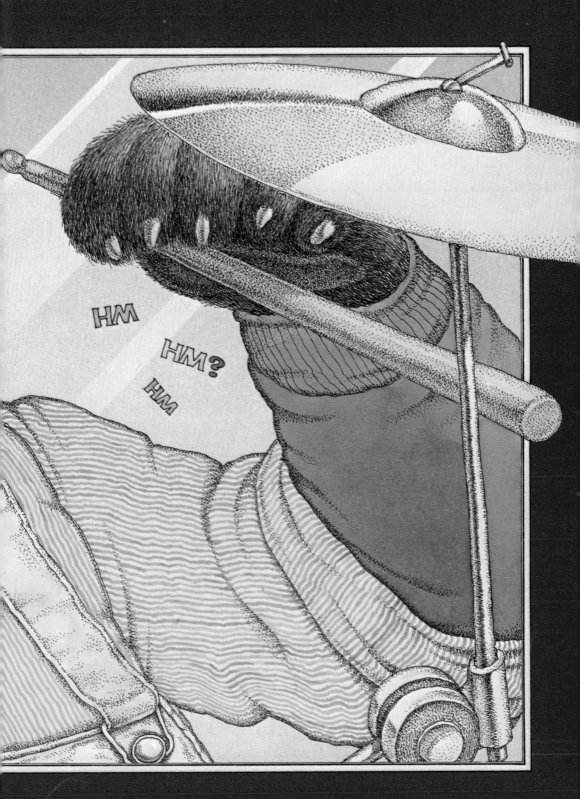

So he takes out the gum.

No!

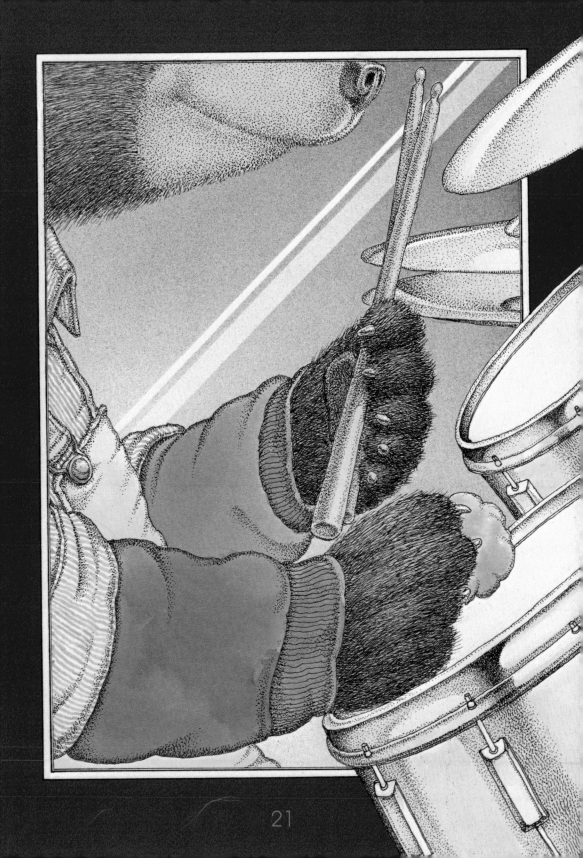

Not there!

Not on the drum!

Never, never
put gum on a drum.

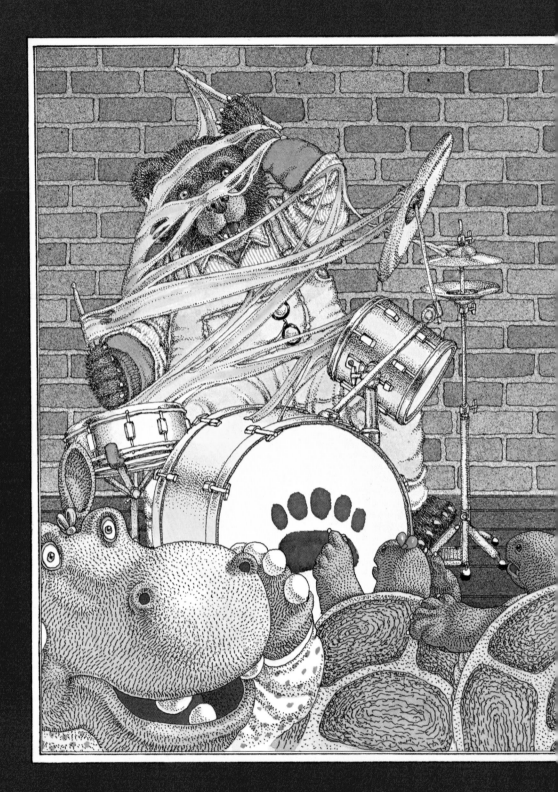

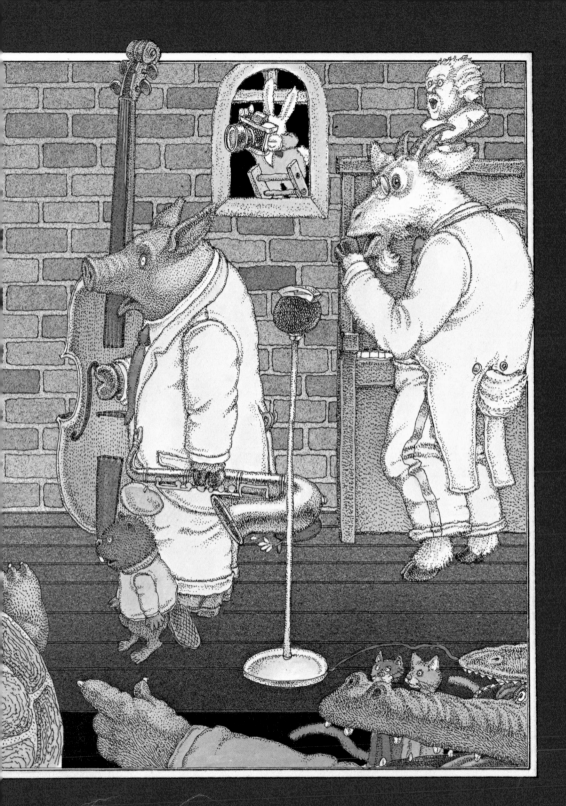

Look at what was done!